Soccer

• An Introduction to Being a Good Sport •

by Aaron Derr

illustrations by Scott Angle

RED
CHAIR
•PRESS•

Start Smart books are published by Red Chair Press

Red Chair Press LLC   PO Box 333   South Egremont, MA 01258-0333

www.redchairpress.com

Publisher's Cataloging-In-Publication Data

Names: Derr, Aaron. | Angle, Scott, illustrator.

Title: Soccer : an introduction to being a good sport / by Aaron Derr ; illustrations by Scott Angle.

Description: South Egremont, MA : Red Chair Press, [2017] | Start smart: sports | Interest age level: 005-009. | Includes Fast Fact sidebars, a glossary and references for additional reading. | Includes bibliographical references and index. | Summary: "Playing a sport is good exercise and fun, but being part of a team is more fun for everyone when you know the rules of the game and how to be a good sport. Soccer, or football as it's known in much of the world, is by far the world's most popular team sport for both boys and girls. In this book, readers learn the history of the game and the role of various positions on the field."-- Provided by publisher.

Identifiers: LCCN 2016934115 | ISBN 978-1-63440-132-6 (library hardcover) | ISBN 978-1-63440-138-8 (paperback) | ISBN 978-1-63440-144-9 (ebook)

Subjects: LCSH: Soccer--Juvenile literature. | Sportsmanship--Juvenile literature. CYAC: Soccer. | Sportsmanship.

Classification: LCC GV943.25 .D47 2017 (print) | LCC GV943.25 (ebook) | DDC 796.334--dc23

Illustration credits: Scott Angle; technical charts by Joe LeMonnier

Photo credits: Cover p. 8, 11, 17, 27, 28, 29, 30, 31: Shutterstock; p. 5, 7: Dreamstime; p. 32: Courtesy of the author, Aaron Derr

This series first published by:
Red Chair Press LLC   PO Box 333   South Egremont, MA 01258-0333

Printed in the United States of America

Distributed in the U.S. by Lerner Publisher Services. www.lernerbooks.com

1116 1P CGBS17

Table of Contents

Words in **bold type** are
defined in the glossary.

CHAPTER 1

Going to Practice

It's the first soccer practice of the season, and Sophie is ready to go! She has played other sports before, but this will be her first time to play soccer, and Sophie can't wait to score a **goal**.

When the practice begins, Sophie's coach talks to the players about how important it is to work together as a team. Each of them will have an important job to do. They all need to try their best if they're going to have a chance to win.

Sophie leans over to her friend Brian and says, "When do we get to score goals?"

"Shhh!" Brian says. "Listen to your coach!"

Sophie's coach tells the players that they need to **warm up** before practice. He asks each player to **jog** around the field one time. Then they all have to do 10 **jumping jacks**.

"When do we get to practice scoring goals?" Sophie asks Brian.

"Shhh!" Brian says.

CHAPTER 2

Passing and Dribbling

Sophie already knows the basic rules of soccer. All of the players on one team try to kick the ball into the other team's goal. And all of the players on the other team try to stop them.

But instead of having them kick the ball into the goal, Sophie's coach asks the players first to practice **dribbling**.

"When do we get to score goals?" Sophie asks Brian.

But Brian is already working on his dribbling.

DID YOU KNOW?

The sport that we call "soccer" is known throughout most of the world as "football." A set of rules called "Association Football" was formed more than 150 years ago. By the time that sport started to become popular in the United States, we already had a game called "football," so "Association Football" became "soccer." Now, what we call "football" is known as either "American football" or "gridiron" in the rest of the world. So confusing!

In soccer, dribbling is when you kick the ball forward with your feet. If you kick the ball too far, the other team will kick it away. That's why it's important to keep the ball close to your feet.

Sophie's coach sets up bright orange cones all along the field. Then he asks all of the players to dribble the ball back and forth between the cones.

FUN FACT

Most soccer players wear **shin** guards. These are important, because when a bunch of players are trying to kick the ball at the same time, it's easy for somebody to accidentally get kicked in the shin. Ouch!

Brian runs as fast as he can between the cones while still keeping the ball close to his feet.

When it gets to be Sophie's turn, she's in such a hurry that she kicks the ball too far away.

"Try to keep the ball closer to your feet, Sophie," her coach says.

"OK," she says. "But when do we get to score goals?"

Next, the coach asks the players to work on **passing**. In soccer, you pass the ball by kicking it with the side of your foot to one of your **teammates**. This is a very important skill. Sometimes your teammate might have a better chance to score than you do.

Sophie and Brian line up and pass the ball back and forth to each other. Brian kicks the ball softly to Sophie, but when Sophie kicks it back it goes too far away. Brian has to run back and get it.

"Try to kick the ball straight to your teammate, Sophie," the coach says.

Sophie looks at Brian.

"When do we get to score goals?" she asks.

DID YOU KNOW?

If a player kicks the ball out of bounds along a sideline, the other team gets to throw it back in. If a player kicks it out next to the other team's goal, the other team gets a **free kick** from a special spot near the front of the goal. And if a player kicks it out next to his own goal, the other team gets a free kick from the corner.

CHAPTER 3

The First Game

Finally, it's time to play a real soccer game. Sophie has her uniform, her shoes and her shin guards. She's ready to go.

But when the game starts, Sophie's coach only sends some of the players out to the field. The rest have to wait on the **sideline** for their turn to play. Sophie is one of the ones who has to wait.

When the game starts, most of the players on the sideline are cheering for their teammates. Brian makes a great pass and one of his teammates scores a goal! The players on the field celebrate. Even the players on the sideline are happy.

Except for Sophie.

"When do I get to score a goal?" she asks.

FUN FACT

The World Cup is an **international** soccer **tournament** with the best teams in the world. Brazil has won the men's World Cup five times, more than any other country. The United States has won the most women's World Cup titles with three championships.

A few minutes later, Sophie finally gets to go into the game.

"Remember, Sophie," her coach says. "Dribble the ball close to your feet, and pass the ball to your teammates when you can."

Sophie runs out to the field. When the ball comes to her, she kicks it forward as hard as she can. She can't wait to score a goal!

"Sophie! Sophie! I'm open!" Brian yells from other side of the field.

Sophie looks over and sees that Brian is standing all by himself in front of the other team's goal. But Sophie wants to score herself, so she tries to dribble closer and…

Suddenly, one of the players from the other team kicks the ball away! The other player dribbles down the field, and then passes it to one of her teammates. Then they pass it again and again and again. Then in an instant, the other team scores a goal!

Sophie is sad. She feels like it's her fault that the other team scored.

Most soccer leagues use referees to make sure the players don't break the rules. If a player makes a small mistake, the other team gets a free kick. If a player makes a bigger mistake, he might be shown a Yellow Card, which acts as a warning. If a player gets two Yellow Cards in one game, he or she has to quit playing in that game. If a player tries to hurt another player, he could receive a Red Card, which means he has to quit the game right away.

"It's OK, Sophie," her coach says. "Next time just remember to keep the ball close to you and pass it to your teammate when you can."

Sophie has a lot to think about.

CHAPTER 4

Back to Work

Sophie decides she needs to practice to get better.

So she goes home and starts kicking the ball around her backyard. Instead of kicking it as hard as she can, she works on dribbling. Back and forth and all around her yard she goes.

Then she works on passing. She aims for a tree in her yard and tries to kick the ball straight at it. It takes a lot of practice, but soon she can kick it right at the tree almost every time.

At the next practice, Sophie is ready to do her best.

Her coach talks to the players about the different **positions** in soccer. He tells them how some of the players are supposed to score goals, and some of them are supposed to stop the other team from scoring a goal.

SOCCER PLAYERS

Professional soccer teams use 11 players at a time. Most kids' teams use eight players.

Goalkeeper: As long as he stays in front of his own goal, the goalkeeper is the only player who can touch the ball with his hands while the game is going on. He wears a different jersey from his teammates so the referee can tell him apart.

Defenders: These players mostly stay in front of the goalkeeper and help keep the ball out of their team's goal.

Midfielders: These players usually stay in the middle of the field. They can go back to help the defenders, and they can also move up to help the forwards.

Forwards: These players can move all the way to the other team's goal. With help from the midfielders, they try to score goals for their team. These players are also called strikers.

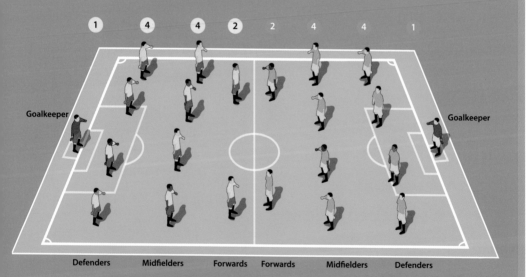

Sophie's coach tells her she'll be playing as a defender. That means her role isn't to score a goal. Her role is to stay back by her team's goal and kick the ball away if one of the players from the other team gets too close.

It's a very important job, and Sophie is excited. After all, a soccer team can't win if the other team scores too many goals!

Sophie's coach says if any of the players try to do something they aren't supposed to do, it hurts the whole team. If someone who is playing defender tries to run too far up the field and score a goal, then there's nobody left to play defender.

Everyone one on the team is counting on each other to do their part.

During practice, Sophie works on doing her part.
She likes keeping the ball away from her team's goal.
When the ball gets too close, she dribbles it away, then
she passes it to one of her teammates so they can try
to score a goal.

"Great job, Sophie!" her coach says.

"Yeah, Sophie," says Brian. "Good job!"

DID YOU KNOW?

Throughout most the world, soccer games are called
matches, and soccer fields are called pitches.

At the next game, Sophie has to start on the sideline. But that's OK. When you're on the sideline, you can still help by cheering on your teammates.

A few minutes into the game, Brian dribbles the ball close to the other team's goal. Then he passes it to his teammate, and she scores!

Sophie cheers.

"Great pass, Brian!" she says.

"Sophie!" her coach says. "It's your turn to play."

Sophie runs onto the field.

CHAPTER 5

Helping the Team

As a defender, Sophie knows she has to stay close to her team's own goal. She lines up and is ready to go.

When the ball gets closer to the other team's goal, Sophie and the other defenders move up in case their teammates need their help. When the ball comes back toward them, they move back to protect their goal.

Sophie's team is doing great. They're winning the game by one goal. But suddenly it looks like the other team might score!

Sophie runs back to try to stop them. A player from the other team is dribbling toward the goal, but the ball goes too far away from him. Sophie kicks it away!

Then Sophie starts dribbling up the field. She sees Brian open up ahead, so she passes the ball straight to him. Great pass!

JUST JOKING!

Q: How do soccer players stay cool in the summer?

A: They stand near the fans!

Brian takes the ball and passes it to another teammate. Before you know it, their team has scored!

"Great pass, Sophie!" Brian says.

"Thanks!" says Sophie. "You did pretty good, too."

After the game, Brian tells Sophie, "I'm sorry you didn't get to score a goal."

"That's OK," Sophie says. "I'll get to score a goal someday. I just like doing my part to help the team."

The only way to become a good soccer player is to practice. Start by kicking a ball in your backyard or any grassy area. It doesn't have to be a real soccer ball! Any ball will do as long as it's big enough to kick around.

When you're just getting started, don't try to kick it hard. It's more important that you're able to control the ball.

Run back and forth and all around, keeping the ball close to you at all times. As you get used to it, try to go faster and faster, always keeping the ball close.

When you get really good, practice keeping your head up so you aren't looking down at the ball the whole time. It's a lot easier to see where you're going when you're looking up!

Glossary

dribbling: moving the ball up the field with your feet

free kick: when a player is allowed to kick the ball without a defender in front of him

goal: when a player kicks the ball into the other team's goal

international: anything that happens between more than one country

jog: running slowly

jumping jacks: an exercise where you jump up and down while moving your arms and legs apart and then together again

open: when a player has no one from the other team around him

passing: kicking the ball to one of your teammates

positions: the place where a player starts the game

shin: the lower, front part of the leg below the knee and above the foot

sideline: the area off to the side of the field

teammates: any of the players on the same team

tournament: a series of games with more than two teams

warm up: exercises that help get a player ready for a practice or a game

What Did You Learn?

See how much you learned about soccer. Answer *true* or *false* for each statement below. Write your answers on a separate piece of paper.

1. When a player kicks the ball into the other team's goal, this is called a point.
   True or false?

2. The goalkeeper is the only player who can use his hands.
   True or false?

3. When dribbling the ball in soccer, it's important to kick it as hard as you can, even if it goes far out in front of you.
   True or false?

4. The defender's job is to help keep the ball out of his or her team's own goal.
   True or false?

5. Soccer fields are shaped like a square.
   True or false?

Answers: 1. False (This is called a goal!), 2. True, 3. False (It's important to keep the ball close to you while dribbling.), 4. True, 5. False. (Soccer fields are shaped like a rectangle.)

For More Information

Books

Bazemore, Suzanne. *Soccer: How It Works* (SI for Kids).
Capstone Press, 2010.

Crisfield, Deborah W. *The Everything Kids' Soccer Book, 3rd Edition.*
Adams Media, 2015.

Forest, Christopher. *Play Soccer Like a Pro* (SI for Kids).
Capstone Press, 2010.

Hoena, Blake. *Everything Soccer.* National Geographic Kids, 2014.

Places

There are several soccer-specific stadiums in North America
you may visit.

Mapfre Stadium, Columbus, Ohio. First soccer-only stadium built
for a professional team. Home of the Columbus Crew.

NSC Stadium, Blaine, Minnesota. Part of the National Sports Center.
Home of Minnesota United FC.

Stade Saputo, Montreal, Quebec. Built on the grounds of the 1976
Summer Olympics. Home of the Montreal Impact.

Web Sites

American Youth Soccer Organization,
oldest youth soccer program in the U.S.
http://www.ayso.org

Official site of Major League Soccer with
news and player information
http://www.mlssoccer.com

Official site of The Fédération Internationale de
Football Association (FIFA)
http://www.fifa.com

Home of news and player information for the U.S. Mens'
and Womens' National teams
http://www.ussoccer.com

Note to educators and parents: Our editors have carefully reviewed these web sites to ensure they are suitable for children. Web sites change frequently, however, and we cannot guarantee that a site's future contents will continue to meet our high standards of quality and educational value. You may wish to preview these sites and closely supervise children whenever they access the Internet.

Index

About the Author

Aaron Derr Aaron Derr is a writer based just outside of Dallas, Texas. He has more than 15 years of experience writing and editing magazines and books for kids of all ages. When he's not reading or writing, Aaron enjoys watching and playing sports, and being a good sport with his wife and two kids.